Playing at

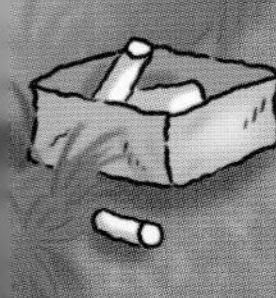

Look at me.

Come and play
on the swings.

Look at me.

Come and play
on the slide.

Look at me.

Come and play
on the horse.

Look at me.

Come and play
on the snail.

Look at me.

Come and play

in the sandbox.

Look at me.

Come and play in the tunnel.

Look at me.

Come and play
in the boat.

Look at me.

Come and play

in the tent.